Christmas '05

To Brody

From Bobby

Library of Congress Cataloging-in-Publication data has been applied for.

ISBN: 0–8109–5044–8

Text and illustrations copyright © 2004 Graeme Base

Published in 2004 by Harry N. Abrams, Incorporated, New York.
All rights reserved. No part of the contents of this book may be
reproduced without the written permission of the publisher.

Printed and bound by Imago Productions, Singapore
10 9 8 7 6 5 4 3 2 1

Harry N. Abrams, Inc.
100 Fifth Avenue
New York, NY 10011
www.abramsbooks.com

Abrams is a subsidiary of

LA MARTINIÈRE
GROUPE

Jungle Drums

Graeme Base

For Kate

Harry N. Abrams, Inc., Publishers

This is *Ngiri Mdogo*. Small, isn't he?
He's the *Smallest Warthog* in Africa.

These are the Bigger Warthogs. They tease Ngiri about being so small. But that's only because they're jealous of the Other Animals who live across the River, with their stunning spots and striking stripes, impressive horns and curly trunks, graceful necks and gorgeous plumage.

Here are the Other Animals who live across the River.
Aren't they just GORGEOUS?

Every year the Other Animals hold a Grand Parade with prizes for the most beautiful. The Warthogs don't even bother entering — mud wrestling isn't on the program.

Tired of being teased, Ngiri heads across the River to play with the Other Animals.

They are arguing among themselves about who is the most beautiful. They turn and stare at Ngiri.

"No spots?" laughs Chui the Leopard.

"No stripes?" whinnies Punda Milia the Zebra.

"Look at those silly little horns!" snorts Kifaru the Rhino.

"He hasn't even got a trunk," trumpets Tembo the Elephant.

"Or a neck," scoffs Twiga the Giraffe.

"Isn't he just the ugliest thing you've ever seen?" crows Ndege the Crested Crane. "And small too!"

They all laugh out loud.

Ngiri heads for home. He is NOT HAPPY.

On the way, he meets Old Nyumbu the Wildebeest, the oldest
and wisest animal in the jungle.

"I hate being so small," he tells her. "Everyone teases me."

Old Nyumbu gets out a little set of bongos.

"These are magic drums," she says. "If you play them, they will
give you whatever you wish for. Do you want them?"

"Oh, yes!" cries Ngiri. "I do!"

He takes the drums in eager hooves.

Old Nyumbu has a twinkle in her eye. "Just remember," she says,
"wishes can come true, but not always as you expect!"

And she gently fades into the bushes.

The sound of Jungle Drums throbs through the night.

But in the morning, despite all his wishing, little Ngiri is still exactly the same.

Then he hears a commotion in the Jungle. The Other Animals have woken to find their stunning spots and striking stripes, impressive horns and curly trunks, graceful necks and gorgeous plumage have all disappeared!

And they are VERY UPSET about it.

The Warthogs, meanwhile, have woken up with stunning spots and striking stripes, impressive horns and curly trunks, graceful necks and gorgeous plumage.

They think they look just FABULOUS!

"Here's Ngiri Mdogo," they laugh as he trots up. "Small as ever — and oh so plain. But we are just like the Other Animals now! We're going to enter the Grand Parade and teach them a lesson in Jungle Style."

When the Other Animals learn on the jungle grapevine that the Warthogs are going to enter the Grand Parade, they are horrified. "Look at us," they cry in dismay. "Those awful Warthogs will win every prize. It will be a complete DISASTER!"

They try making fake markings out of sticks and grass and colored mud. But it all washes off in the evening downpour.

The Warthogs parade along the Riverbank in their newfound finery.

"You stole our markings," yell the Other Animals. "Give them back!"

"They're not your markings, they're ours," snort the Warthogs. "They fell from the sky. And now WE are the most beautiful animals in the Jungle."

"They belong to us," growl the Other Animals. "If you don't give them back before the Grand Parade, we will come and TAKE THEM!"

Poor Ngiri. What has he done?

The wild African moon comes up, and Jungle Drums beat out
again across the Savannah.

It's still dark as Ngiri creeps over to where the Other Animals are sleeping. He breathes a sigh of relief to see stunning spots and striking stripes, impressive horns and curly trunks, graceful necks and gorgeous plumage. Then the Animals stir and sit up.

THE MARKINGS ARE ON THE WRONG ANIMALS!

"It's the Warthogs who have done this," cry the Other Animals.
"THEY'VE PUT A SPELL ON US!"

They stomp off angrily across the River.

Meanwhile, the Warthogs are in a terrible state.

"What's happened to my nose?"

"What's happened to my neck?"

"How can I roll in the mud with all these feathers?"

"I can't run with this great long trunk. I'll end up as someone's dinner for sure."

The Warthogs have become even more like the Other Animals they admire so much.

"THEY'VE PUT A SPELL ON US!"

They stomp off angrily across the River.

"What have you done to us?" demand the Warthogs.
"What have you done to us?" demand the Other Animals.
Everyone is shouting at once.

"Stop it!" cries Ngiri Mdogo in a squeaky voice. "It was me."
All the animals stop and look at him in amazement. He tells
them about the magic drums.

"I made a wish. Two wishes, in fact, though they went wrong. I wanted you all to stop teasing me. But I didn't mean for you to start fighting. Why can't you all be happy the way you are?"

"Because we look RIDICULOUS!" says everyone together. "We want to be the way we WERE!"

"Well . . ." says Ngiri thoughtfully. "If you'd all be happier that way, I suppose I could try making one more wish . . ."

For a third time, the sound of Jungle Drums echoes
through the still night air.

As the sun rises over the rim of the world, the Warthogs and the Other Animals wake and look around with relief. They are all back to normal.

But Ngiri Mdogo sighs. After all that trouble, he is still exactly the same — the Smallest Warthog in Africa.

Something *has* changed, though. No one is teasing him any more. The Bigger Warthogs and the Other Animals look at Ngiri, then at each other. Then they shrug.

"So what if he's the littlest? Someone has to be."

That evening, the Grand Parade goes ahead as usual. The Other Animals who live across the River show off their stunning spots and striking stripes, impressive horns and curly trunks, graceful necks and gorgeous plumage. The Warthogs clap and cheer.

Then the Warthogs put on a mud-wrestling display, including a very clever mud pyramid with a mud fountain, and the Other Animals clap and cheer.

Then Ngiri does a drum solo (but is very careful not to wish for anything, just in case) and EVERYONE claps and cheers!

And the night is a Roaring Success.

THE END

Was everything really back to normal in the Jungle?

The Warthogs were still not quite the way they had been before Ngiri made his wishes. And neither were the Other Animals. In fact, if you look very carefully, you will find that every creature watching and listening from the trees changed after Ngiri played his magic drums.

Look even closer and you might also find Old Nyumbu the Wildebeest hidden somewhere on every spread.

Back into the Jungle we go!

A note on Swahili pronunciation

Some of the names in *Jungle Drums* are a bit tricky to pronounce. They are actually the Swahili words for the animals.

Ngiri Mdogo (Little Warthog)

Make the sound of a small "n" then say "giri" right after it: "nnngiri." Do the same with Mdogo "mmmdohgo." Ngiri means "warthog" and Mdogo means "little." In Swahili, you say the name of the thing first, then the word describing it.

Chui (Leopard)

This one sounds the way it looks: "chewy." Just right for a leopard!

Punda Milia (Zebra)

Sounds like "poondah meeleah." Punda means "donkey" and Milia means "stripes" — so a zebra is a "donkey with stripes."

Kifaru (Rhino)

Sounds the way it looks: "ki-farooo."

Tembo (Elephant)

This sounds the way it looks too: "tem-bo."

Twiga (Giraffe)

Pronounced "tweegah."

Ndege (Crested Crane)

Similar to Ngiri with a small "n" at the start: "nnndehgeh." Ndege actually means "bird." In Swahili, they don't have names for different birds; they tend to say "bird," then add something to describe it. Unfortunately my Swahili is pretty limited so "Ndege" will have to do!

Nyumbu (Wildebeest)

Pronounced in two syllables: "newm-boo."

Have fun!

[signature]

Answers to the Hidden Animal Puzzle and other Jungle Secrets: There are twelve animals watching from the trees. They each appear four times, changed slightly every time Ngiri plays the drums. They are: Monkey (number of stripes on tail); Kingfisher (color of beak); Hyena (number of stripes on forehead); Caterpillar (number of legs); Hornbill (pattern on bill); Dragonfly (body color); Antelope (shape of horns); Beetle (number of spots); Snake (skin pattern); Chameleon (shape of markings); Aardvark (color of ears); Snail (number of spirals). You can also find Old Nyumbu the Wildebeest somewhere on every page, watching over Ngiri — sometimes just her head, sometimes her whole body. As for the changes that stay with the Warthogs and the Other Animals at the end — the eyes have it!